To Carol,

Thank you for
treating me like royalty.
Your support and encouragem[ent]
have been invaluable.
You are truly a woman
of substance.

Love,
Kathie

The Portly Princess of Thynneland

Kathleen Marie Marsh

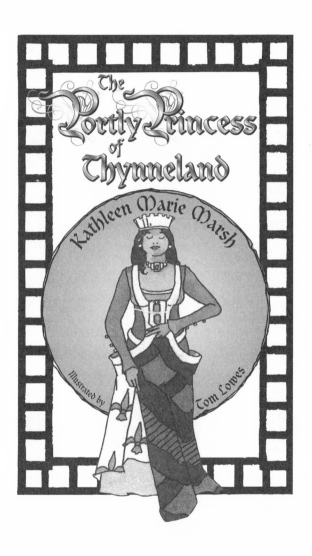

Illustrated by Tom Lowes

Goblin Fern Press
Madison, Wisconsin

The Portly Princess of Thynneland

For information or to order additional copies please contact
Goblin Fern Press
3809 Mineral Point Road, Madison, WI 53705
www.goblinfernpress.com
Toll-free: 888-670-BOOK (2665)

ISBN 1-59598-016-4

First printing June 2004
Printed in the United States
10 9 8 7 6 5 4 3 2 1

Dedication

To my noble daughter,
a true woman of substance

Acknowledgements

Writing this book has been one of the greatest learning experiences of my life. I wish to thank my husband Jon for his support and encouragement, my friend Heather Sprangers for her editorial eagle eye, my sister Carol Roche for her insightful marketing advice, and my sister Sharon Brantmeier for leading me to Goblin Fern Press. I also want to express my heartfelt appreciation to Kira Henschel and Drew Burns at GFP for believing in me, and to Tom Lowes for making my characters come alive with his wonderful illustrations. I must also thank Melvin Powers of Welshire Books, who introduced me to this very special form of story-telling.

Preface

With obesity at epidemic proportions in America, attention is being given to one of the root causes: poor eating habits acquired in earliest childhood. What role do parents have in establishing their children's life-long eating patterns? The Portly Princess of Thynneland addresses the issue, not with sermons and scolding, but with an entertaining story whose moral should not be lost amid the humor and romance of this grown-up fairy tale.

Sveltelanna Castle

in

Thynneland

Chapter 1

Once upon a time there lived a fashionably thin King and Queen whose domain was the tightly-run Kingdom of Thynneland. They lived in a castle called Sveltelanna and ruled with a slender, iron hand. However, Rollo and Reeda were a kind and benevolent pair who generally viewed their subjects much as a fat-farm might regard its less-than-enthusiastic clients. Every law, indeed every facet of life in Thynneland, was designed to support their conviction that thin people are happy people, so all public policy was fashioned to keep Thynnelanders slim, trim, toned and fit.

From a child's earliest kindergarten years to graduation from Royal University, all school curriculum was embedded with a physical fitness theme. Nutrition, health and exercise were required subjects in every academic institution in the realm. Junk food and alcoholic beverages were absolutely forbidden, sweet treats being reserved for special celebrations. Mid-morning and mid-afternoon exercise breaks were compulsory, with all citizens required to elevate their heart rates twice daily for twenty minutes.

To ensure full compliance with the Anti-Obesity Act, every subject had to report to the Ministry of Public Appearance once each year to be weighed and measured. Anyone over the age of eighteen who was not within twenty pounds of his or her ideal weight as determined on the official Government Fat-Ratio Index was immediately sent off to the Hinterland to work in and eat from the royal vegetable gardens, weeding, hoeing and fertilizing until ideal weight was achieved and the offender allowed to go home.

There was one notable exception. Muscular young men were permitted to audition for the Thynneland Whackers, the King's personal leatherball team. If a young man made the team, he was allowed to gain weight at will, but must be able on summer Sunday afternoons to knock opposing leatherball players senseless. It was common knowledge that sumptuous meals were served at the team's training table, and huge boxes of the King's favorite candy, butternut creams, were awarded to those players who sent an opponent to the infirmary on a stretcher.

Years passed and the perennially slim inhabitants of Thynneland lived happily and healthily. Well, almost. Truth be told, many Thynnelanders, especially those living in Sveltelanna, found they couldn't maintain perfect self-control. Lapses occurred more and more frequently, but excesses were ignored as long as individuals were able to fit within "girth guidelines" at the annual weigh-ins. Queen Reeda's weight, however, never varied more than a pound or two. She would have voiced her concern to Rollo about Thynneland's growing relaxation of the rules, but he was one of the kingdom's most flagrant violators, so she kept still.

Thus, life went on uneventfully until one crisp autumn morning when the Queen, who felt an emptiness in her innards not related to food, petitioned the King for a private audience to discuss her desire to start a family. The King, who could never say no to a woman he loved, acquiesced at once.

A year later, the couple giddily celebrated the birth of their first child, a daughter they named Volumina because she arrived on the night of the full harvest moon, a fact to which her mother always attributed her daughter's tendency to do everything to the fullest possible extent, especially when it came to eating.

Even at birth, Volumina was, to the Queen's conster-
nation, a chubby baby. Her little arms and legs
resembled links of plump sausages, and her wet-nurse
soon learned what a challenge it is to string any sort of
bib around a child who has several chins. The Queen,
distraught at the thought of Volumina growing up with
a "weight problem," discussed it privately with
Quackum, the Royal Physician.

"Could some obesity gene lurk in Rollo's contribution
to our daughter's genetic profile?" she asked bluntly.

"It's possible, Your Majesty," Quackum replied, carefully choosing his answer out of fear that he might offend
the King and lose his position. "But do not worry. We have
a wide array of potions and spells to use in the event that
the Princess does indeed tend toward corpulence.
However, since these regimens have not been tested on
children, I suggest we wait and see if this is something she
will outgrow."

The Queen agreed, but nevertheless did her best to get
her daughter off to a good, thin start. Volumina was
weaned to the cup at six months and that cup, of course,
contained fat-free milk. When the Princess cried out for
more filling fare, the Queen let her bellow, figuring that

since crying requires considerable effort, it must therefore efficiently burn calories.

But the King, who had never mastered the art of ignoring hunger pangs, took a very different view of the matter. It was widely known but never openly discussed that Rollo loved to eat and gained as much as forty pounds each winter. However, he always reached goal weight by his birth date anniversary, All Saints Day. It took considerable effort; he had to joust, swordfight and swim the moat several hours per day, but on the First of November, his weight was right on target. (This, of course, meant he gave himself permission to overindulge during the Holidays and the long, boring winter months ahead).

So it was that Rollo took pity on his hungry little daughter. He couldn't stand to see Volumina frown, much less hear her whimpering and wailing. Once she started solids, the King secretly instructed the nurse to defy his wife's decree. "For God's sake, Margareete, mix some cream into the Princess's porridge," he ordered. "Can't you see the child's hungry?"

"It's her birthday, for God's sake. . .

If cake is what she wants,

let her eat cake."

Chapter 2

Her appetite now assuaged, Volumina was content and began "filling out," sleeping peacefully through the night. While the Queen fretted over her daughter's growing pudginess, it was impossible not to notice that, despite her rolls of baby fat, Volumina was actually quite beautiful. She had creamy white skin, shiny thick raven-black hair and immense gray eyes framed by lush ebony lashes. The Queen didn't mind taking credit for her daughter's comely countenance, but bristled when visiting dignitaries would remark, "Why, Your Majesty, she looks just like you!"

"She does have my *facial* features," the Queen would retort in a defensive tone, and if they were at all observant, admirers knew enough to nod, smile and let it go at that.

Days passed into weeks and weeks into months. As all good parents do, the Royal couple went into the nursery each evening to check on their daughter and kiss her good night. Determined to quickly regain her pre-pregnancy figure, the Queen would then retire to her chamber to crunch out a hundred sit-ups. Meanwhile, the King, who was a bit ahead of his time in believing girls should be reared to assume even the loftiest of positions, thought it never too early to start career education. He spent a few minutes each night quietly going over affairs of state with the baby. Volumina would just look at him with her huge knowing eyes, and the King was absolutely convinced she was taking it all in.

One night, in an inexplicable lapse of judgment, the King filched a sweetcake from the leatherball larder to smuggle in to his little daughter. Taking a tentative bite of the tiny cake, Volumina's taste buds experienced "sweet" for the first time. She squealed with delight at the pleasurable sensation cascading over her tongue, and her fate was sealed. The King, who knew well the delicious decadence of dessert, smiled broadly at the Princess's reaction and felt a deep sense of fulfillment as he fed her.

The building process, even if it involves creating a "sweet tooth," takes time, and in this case it escalated slowly. . . a honey biscuit here, an oatmeal raisin scone there. The King did not consider his behavior to be corruption on any level. Indeed, he loved his daughter with the innocent emotion that only a pure, if misguided, heart can hold. He beamed with pride as her blind trust grew into affection, affection into hero worship. His heart soared when she cooed as he squeezed her chubby arms; when she giggled as he called her "Plumpkin" or "Butterball."

As the months passed, the King became more and more brazen, sneaking Volumina sweetcakes and buttercream candies whenever his wife was away, perhaps having her hair styled or visiting the royal seamstress for a fitting on yet another size 4 gown. When he actually took the time to consider what he was doing, Rollo pushed his guilty thoughts away, positive that Volumina would one day outgrow her baby fat, but never the adoration for her father that he was now nurturing. He even rationalized his behavior by telling himself that he too slipped from time to time, surreptitiously stealing away from the palace for a night of carousing with a group of high-living young lords in a neighboring fiefdom. (These daring but marvelous escapades featured pints of heavy ale, knockwurst, cheese curds and honey pecan tarts, with buttercream candies for munching on the long horseback ride home).

As the anniversary of her birth approached, Volumina took her first steps on two wobbly, fat little legs. The Royal Physician, whose worst fear was not in being declared incompetent, but in being found irrelevant, reassured the Queen. "Now that the Princess is walking, the weight will just melt away."

Quackum's prediction would most likely have been accurate, but the King, who was hopelessly addicted to the hero-worship in his daughter's large, luminous eyes, continued his nocturnal visits to the nursery. Thus, by her third birthday, when she was allowed to sit at the royal table for the first time, Volumina weighed nearly three stone, a little over 50 pounds.

A huge celebration was held to mark the third anniversary of Volumina's birth. At dinner, the Queen was beside herself when her daughter sniffed disdainfully at the vegetarian platter set before her and instead downed three butterbuns slathered in apple currant jelly. When told she had to finish her vegan plate before getting any birthday cake, Volumina threw her first royal temper tantrum.

Much to the Queen's dismay, the King picked up his screaming, kicking daughter, set her on his knee, and placed a large piece of cake in front of her. "It's her birthday, for God's sake," he said a little too sharply as the Queen silently glared at him. "It's only once a year. If cake is what she wants, let her eat cake."

"You didn't mean to hurt her,

did you, Plumpkin?

Now tell your sister

you're sorry and you love her."

Chapter 3

ike the woman who declared, "I have so much to do, I don't know where to start so I'm going to bed," the Queen turned a blind eye to Volumina's problem. "When there's nothing to be done, it's best to do nothing," counseled the Royal Physician. "Once the Princess starts school, she will be too busy to eat and the weight will melt away."

The situation thus went into a holding pattern until one day early the next spring when the Queen awoke to the loud ticking of her biological clock. She decided to bypass the petitioning process this time and instead brazenly seduced her husband. Delighted by Reeda's spontaneous (and rare) passion, the King immediately granted his royal favors. Nine months later, as a seasonably cold December day dawned, their second daughter, Demura, was born.

Unlike her older sister, Demura was a fair, blue-eyed child who most resembled her father, except that she was fine-boned and delicate like her mother. She was also a much more demanding child than Volumina had ever been; colicky, fussy, and unable to establish any kind of reasonable sleep schedule. She rejected the royal wet-nurse from the first feeding, forcing the Queen to nurse her baby herself.

Because this necessitated that Reeda move Demura into her private chambers, Volumina was escorted there by her father to meet her baby sister a few days after the child was born. Volumina had been repeatedly told by adults she trusted that a baby sister would add to her quality of life. Nevertheless, she eyed the new Princess suspiciously. What she observed was a screaming, smelly, helpless being who was doted upon with attention previously reserved for her alone. Of course she immediately concluded this new arrival was a new RIVAL and promptly pinched the inter-loper's cheek much too hard when she was allowed near.

"Stop!" Reeda cried. "You must be gentle with your baby sister."

"She didn't mean to hurt her," the King said quickly in his daughter's defense. "You didn't mean to hurt her, did you, Plumpkin? Now tell your sister you're sorry and you love her."

Volumina stared at her father with incredulous eyes. When she realized that he was actually serious, she decided she just wanted this to be over so she could get back to the Jousting Knights picture book she had been studying in the Royal Reading Room.

"Sorry," Volumina mumbled. "Love you," she said, without actually looking at anyone, especially Demura.

"That's a good girl," the King gushed as he wrapped his arms around Volumina in a big bear hug. He had no idea how much his behavior confused the little girl. She was being rewarded for saying words she didn't feel! Nevertheless, she responded hungrily to his approving gesture, feeling completely safe and secure in his fatherly embrace. She shut her eyes and clung to him a long time, basking in the warmth of his affection. The hug felt so good, she wondered why she was unable to banish the accompanying feelings of guilt that were so unpleasant as to be almost painful. Had she been older, Volumina might have realized it was because she had told her first lie.

Twirpin enjoyed

the humiliating process

of publicly calling out

each subject's weight.

Chapter 4

*T*oo young to understand that parental love has no boundaries, Volumina mistook the affection her parents lavished on Demura as a sign of diminished love for her. To compensate for the perceived void, Volumina found her solace in food, especially sweets, which she found easy to procure from Vapid, one particularly gullible leatherball player. Of course, this was all subconscious, but the calories added up anyway.

The Queen had long ago despaired of changing her daughter's "unconventional" eating habits, and was now too busy with the baby to object when Volumina consumed fattening foods. It was as if Reeda had given up on her older daughter and was concentrating her efforts on Demura, where they might have a better chance to succeed. As for the King, he continued to indulge Volumina, who, if truth be told, was his favorite. Like him, she was evolving into a highly intelligent, curious person who made friends easily and was possessed of an insatiable zest for not just food, but LIFE.

Upon turning five, Volumina was deemed ready to begin her formal education. Being of a more liberal persuasion, the King and Queen enrolled their daughter in the Royal Public School. The Princess took to school like a blacksmith to a hot fire. She reveled in learning, enjoying the company of these "common" children and thriving in an atmosphere of intellectual and social challenge.

Five-year-olds are by nature unbiased against all manner of human physical differences and equally impervious to the privilege of status and wealth. Consequently, Volumina's royal blood and heavy body made no impression whatsoever on her classmates. Being intelligent, kind, and genial, not to mention a good sport and a loyal friend who could keep a secret, Volumina became immensely popular at school. (It didn't hurt that she was also a first-rate "sharer" who brought a large bag of buttercream candies to school on a regular basis).

Within three years, the "Big Princess," as the subjects of Thynneland came to call her, was reading chapter books and showed an aptitude for math and social studies that was clearly remarkable. So what that there was now occasional gossip about Volumina's large size? It went unnoticed by her amid the self-fulfillment she was experiencing on a daily basis. She had even come to grips with something she learned was called "sibling rivalry," concluding it best to tolerate her younger sister with good-natured resignation.

Volumina's mature attitude was most opportune because by the time Demura began her formal education, it was apparent that the two sisters were complete opposites. While the younger Princess was not beautiful, she was razor-thin and could eat whatever food she pleased and not gain an ounce of superfluous fat. She was also a quiet, shy girl who rarely smiled and usually chose puzzles and paints over people.

As the years passed, Demura and Volumina tacitly acknowledged their peaceful coexistence, with Demura spending most of her time with her mother while Volumina clearly preferred the company of her father. During her free hours, she could often be found in the Throne Room, where she watched the King use patience and wisdom in dealing with political, social and economic challenges. Her quick wit and engaging manner made her a welcome observer, even though some of the courtiers privately voiced their concerns about her growing girth.

"The Princess has such a beautiful face," remarked the Minister of Social Affairs one day. "What a pity she is so fat."

"Indeed," replied the Minister of Marital Relations, wringing his hands in frustration. "How am I to obtain a suitable marriage partner for her when the time comes?"

"We must seek professional advice," the two agreed and the very next day they paid a visit to Twirpin, the Minister of Weights and Measures. Twirpin was a skinny, beady-eyed, balding man in charge of annual weigh-ins. He enjoyed the humiliating process of publicly calling out each subject's weight, and actually relished the opportunity to send goal weight violators to the Hinterland.

"Why is nothing being done to curtail the Princess's weight?" the two ministers demanded as the meeting with Twirpin began. "Within a few years she will be old enough to marry, and a match profitable to our Kingdom's business interests will be difficult to arrange if her appearance is not improved."

Like many politicians, Twirpin was a hypocrite, and so he scolded his colleagues for their open criticism of the Princess's figure, but self-righteously saw it as his civic duty to request a private audience with the King and the Royal Physician to discuss the matter.

"Your Majesty," the Minister began, more nervous than he expected to be during the ensuing meeting. "Some of us, I mean, some of your ministers are curious as to why the physical stature. . . no, let me rephrase that. . . the physical physique, no, I apologize, Sire. If you will allow me to start over?" He was perspiring profusely and now wished he had sent one of his underlings instead. He took a deep breath and began again.

"Forgive me, Sire, but may I speak freely?" The King nodded and he recklessly plunged ahead.

"Some of your royal advisors are concerned as to why the issue of the physical presence of the Princess Volumina is not being addressed by the Royal Physician," he said, pointing a long, bony finger at the doctor who sat silently beside the King in haughty self-importance. Startled by the accusing gesture, Quackum began to fidget in his chair.

Emboldened by satisfaction at seeing a man he detested sweat, the Minister continued. "There is much concern in the land, Sire. Indeed, your daughter is being referred to in some parts of the realm as the "Portly Princess." He coughed to cover his discomfort at revealing such treasonous information.

A cloud of rage descended upon the King and he gestured to the doctor, whose face turned a ghastly shade of pale. "The Royal Physician has advised me that my daughter is merely 'big boned' and will lose weight easily when, in the biological sense, she becomes a woman." He turned to look directly at Quackum. "Is that not what you have said?"

The Royal Physician, terrified by the King's angry blue eyes burning into his very soul, gulped and said the first thing he could think of. "The law specifically says that a citizen has until age 18 to fit within the required weight guidelines."

"Exactly," said the King as he turned back to the two trembling ministers. "And you may tell those concerned advisors that since my daughter approaches only her twelfth birth date anniversary, she has many years to comply with the edicts of the Thynneland Anti-Obesity Act. Now be on your way before I decide to feed you to the hungry rats in my dungeon!"

On the day

before her eighteenth birthday,

Quackum and all his possessions

were reported missing.

Chapter 5

The King considered the matter settled, but the Royal Physician was more than a trifle alarmed. He sighed with relief a few weeks later when he was called to the castle sleeping quarters. The Princess had awakened with sheets stained by the evidence of her "physical maturity." Surely now his prediction would come true! Of course it did not, but somehow Quackum was able to convince the King and Queen to wait nearly four more years before concluding in despair that not even passing through puberty had solved Volumina's problem.

Thus at the annual weigh-in required upon the beginning of her seventeenth year, Volumina tipped the scales at fifteen stone, well over 200 pounds. Since her full adult height was recorded at 69 inches (nearly four inches taller than her mother and sister, who both weighed under 8 stone), it was determined that she was more than fifty pounds over her maximum target weight of 155.

For her part, Volumina could not help but anguish over the fact that she was clearly obese. (It might have been worse had her father not issued a decree immediately following her weigh-in that all full-length mirrors in the kingdom be taken down and stored until further notice).

So, to everyone's delight but entirely on her own, Volumina decided to limit herself to one "treat" per day. She lost several pounds in a fortnight and was feeling quite satisfied by her efforts. Even the Royal Physician was smiling for the first time in months, clearly delighted to take credit where credit was definitely not due. But then along came the Feast of Christmastide to do him, and the Portly Princess, in. She hadn't the willpower to resist the tables groaning under mountains of holiday goodies that were available only once a year. Despite her good intentions, her hand visited her mouth far too often and she ended up gaining back all she had lost plus more.

Now Quackum grew desperate. Setting out on a holy quest to get his patient down to goal weight, he researched the royal archives for every conceivable spell or potion that offered any kind of hope. Since she coveted a thin figure as much as he did, Volumina cooperated willingly. She concentrated until her eyes ached at the pendulum he swung back and forth in numerous failed attempts at hypnosis. She sat cross-legged until her legs went numb in an unsuccessful effort to meditate away the excess fat. She dutifully swallowed disgusting concoctions, some of which caused her to gag and regurgitate the contents of her stomach. She consumed huge goblets of spring water until the maid complained that she did nothing all day but run to empty the contents of the oft-used chamber pot.

Almost in despair, for one week she ate nothing but vegetables but was forced to abandon that diet when she found herself running to the chamber pot nearly every hour and awakening in the middle of the night with excruciating hunger pangs. With each new regimen she would lose weight, but then was unable to sustain such austerity. After every failed attempt, she would sink deeper into self-hatred and go on an eating binge, which resulted in her gaining it all back with a few added pounds for good measure.

On the day before her eighteenth birthday, when Volumina weighed in at sixteen stone, Quackum and all his possessions were reporting missing. He had simply

vanished, melted away in the middle of the night. No trace of him was to be found, but rumor had it he must have fled in terror, lest he be remanded to the King's dungeon when the scale's verdict proved him an incompetent fool.

The image of a baby

crying from hunger

accessed something

deeply hidden inside Volumina.

Chapter 6

Thus it was that on the day after her eighteenth birthday, Volumina's parents had no choice but to send her to the Hinterland. Since she had never been away from the safety of the castle before, the King instructed that their most trusted lady-in-waiting, Marilee, accompany her. Acting as royal bodyguard was Favo, the King's favorite leatherball player, who had recently celebrated his twenty-second birthday by passing for six touchdowns in a stunning 42-0 victory over the Viscount Vikings.

Favo was a fiercely competitive, chauvinistic man who had been drafted from a poor southern village and risen to the King's highest favor on the strength of his right arm and quick legs. An imposing muscular specimen with a head of curly brown hair, dark brown eyes, and an impish grin that melted all the ladies' hearts, Favo was not happy with his new duties. He disdained being thrust into the companionship of a fat female, but being a consummate team player, knew of no other choice but to obey the King's command. He would escort Volumina to the Hinterland, and should it be necessary, lay down his very life in her defense.

"Your orders are to see that she is safe and comfortable, but other than that, you may use any and all methods to facilitate her weight loss program," the King had commanded Marilee and Favo. "But if any evil befalls my daughter, I shall have a large stone tied to each of your necks and you shall be thrown into the river."

The three-day trip to the Hinterland was exhausting but uneventful. Upon arrival, due to her royal status, Volumina was housed in the best quarters available. She was to be spared working in the gardens and would instead spend her days doing physical conditioning as prescribed by her bodyguard who would also serve as her personal trainer. Her meals would be prepared by Marilee, who would see that only low-fat, low-calorie foods were on the Princess's tray.

Wisely remembering his own youthful indiscretions, the King had ordered that the Princess and Favo be continuously watched, a formality that was entirely unnecessary. From the very first day, the two detested each other, she because he was a strict taskmaster and he because he regarded her body as physically repulsive. Indeed, he seemed to enjoy every opportunity to let her know how much she disgusted him.

"You are nothing but a spoiled, pampered house pet. No wonder you're so fat," he remarked cruelly when she ran less than a quarter mile before collapsing in a sweaty heap.

"You cannot say such things to me. I shall have my father whip you!" she cried.

"Perhaps. But he is not here and I have my orders, Your Majesty. You are my responsibility now."

With nothing to be gained by being stubborn or uncooperative, Volumina set her jaw and opted for peaceful coexistence, just as she had with her sister. Within two weeks she was almost enjoying her daily workouts and the low-calorie meals. Her gowns began to hang upon her slimmer body, and after a month she requested what heretofore would have been unthinkable: she asked to be weighed!

"Under fourteen stone, Your Majesty," Favo reported with grudging admiration. "You've lost over thirty pounds."

"That is near half of what I need to lose," she said happily. "I am determined to return to Sveltelanna by Christmastide."

"That is not likely," he replied, "for the next thirty will be far more difficult. You have a long road ahead."

"Why cannot you extend to me the smallest bit of praise, Favo?" Volumina asked as tears came to her eyes. "Why must you always wound me with your words?"

"Because you are spoiled and enjoy a privileged life that is the result of nothing but an accident of birth." His face reddened and he looked at her with contempt. "Once our work here is finished, you will go home to be married off to a rich prince and live in luxury whilst the people must survive the coming famine."

"Famine? What are you saying?" Her soft gray eyes grew wide.

"You could not bear it if I told you."

"I am stronger than when we first met. I order you to tell me."

"Very well, since I am commanded." He looked her squarely in the eye, something no man except her father had ever done. When he saw the pain lodged there, for the first time his heart softened.

"The snows last winter were sparse and there has been little rain this growing season. The crop that was harvested will not see the kingdom through the winter unless rationing is instituted at once. But that will not happen. Each year the castle and court consume the lion's share of what is produced. We have enjoyed many years of plenty, and there has been always been more than enough to go around. This will not be such a year. I am told that already the peasants in the villages talk of how to quiet the cries of starving children."

The image of babies crying from hunger accessed something deeply hidden in Volumina's memory as Favo continued his tirade. "This year the poor will be left with the scraps so people like you can feast on the fruits of their labor." Again the crushed look in her eyes made him feel sorry he had spoken so harshly.

"My father would never allow such a thing!" she retorted hotly.

"That may be so, however he does not know of the problem. His advisors do not have the courage to report such things to the court."

"Is there nothing to be done?" she asked, again imagining the agonized cries of hungry children.

"No, nothing I can do, but you. . . you are the King's daughter," he replied, impressed by her concern and surprised at the newfound respect he suddenly felt for her.

"You have spoken rightly, Favo. I am the King's daughter, and there is much I can and will do," she said with sudden, deep conviction. "Tell Marilee to pack my things, Favo. We leave for the castle in the morning."

His lips were soft and warm,

his kiss chaste

but holding the promise of so much more.

Chapter 7

The journey back to Sveltelanna took three cold, wet, miserable days. Volumina wondered if they would ever get home. The weather turned bad the afternoon they left, and the cruel December winds whistled and howled, frigid air sneaking like a thief through the cracks in the carriage doors.

Every part of her body was numb, especially her face, which by necessity was exposed to the frosty air. The only time Volumina managed to get warm was when they stopped at a village inn to rest for the night. Marilee brought her a tray of food, but she was too tired to eat. Instead, she sipped the cup of hot broth Favo insisted would take the chill out of her bones and crawled into a bed preheated with warmed rocks. Within minutes, she was snuggled under a thick pile of homespun quilts and fell off to an exhausted, dreamless sleep.

The next two days Favo pushed the traveling party harder than Pozzi, the driver, thought prudent, for Favo was alarmed on two accounts. One, the Princess's welfare was completely in his hands, and his very life depended upon his getting her to the palace safely. The second reason confused and concerned him even more than the first.

It had begun the second morning of their trip when he had gone to deliver Volumina her morning tea. She had appeared at the inn room door enveloped in a patchwork quilt, her waist-length raven tresses a wild mane framing her flawless ivory complexion. In taking the teacup from him, she had brushed his fingertips with hers. When she smiled her thanks for the welcome hot beverage, her gray eyes sparkling, his heart had skipped a beat. He was taken aback at the sudden, unbidden desire rushing through his body. He managed to stammer something about the need to be on their way within the hour and quickly took his leave.

For the entire day Favo debated with himself as to what had occurred. There was no doubt the Princess was stunningly beautiful from the neck up, but her thick middle, wide hips and heavy legs had always made that irrelevant. How was it then that he found himself wanting to take her in his arms and give her what he was completely convinced would be her first real kiss? And what if that were to happen? Was he not a commoner with no right to even kiss her royal heel? Were he to approach her, even if she accepted his advances, would not her father have him executed and order his head be thrust upon a petard and mounted at the castle gates? He finally concluded that he had mistaken his growing feelings of respect for those of love. Just the same, he avoided Volumina all day until the sun was setting.

They were less than a mile from their intended rest stop when ice crystals began pelting the traveling party. Favo knew they must hurry, but deep snow impeded their progress. He was so intent upon getting them to the inn before dark that he ordered Pozzi to push the horses harder. It was too much. One of the huge gray Belgians slipped on the ice and the carriage would have fallen off the steep road had it not gotten stuck in a snowdrift first.

No matter how Pozzi tried, he could not force the horses to pull hard enough to dislodge the carriage. Finally, Favo commanded several of the accompanying soldiers to get behind the carriage and push. They managed to move it a few feet, but the additional weight of their passengers inside was just enough to thwart success.

"If Her Majesty had sense enough to get out, it would lighten the load and we could get the carriage unstuck," Favo finally shouted in frustration.

Marilee gasped at Favo's boldness. Get out of the carriage in a blinding snowstorm? Was he mad to even suggest such a thing? Seeing that the women were not going to cooperate and knowing there was nothing else to be done, Favo opened the carriage door and hoisted himself up into the coach. He muttered a half-hearted apology, then pulled them both to their feet and pushed Marilee out the door into Pozzi's waiting arms. Favo now turned his attention to the Princess. "Pray, Your Highness, please get out," he pleaded.

"I was just about to," she said imperiously, wrapping her heavy cloak tightly about her body and descending with a lofty air, rudely shoving away Pozzi's helping hand.

It worked. Within minutes the carriage was back on the road and an hour later Volumina was sitting beside a blazing fireplace, warming herself with the cup of hot meat broth she had wanted to refuse but grudgingly took from Favo's chapped and calloused hands. Marilee had gone to the carriage to fetch a forgotten piece of baggage, and the Princess found herself alone with a man other than her father for the first time in her life.

"You are fearless, are you not?" she asked him pointedly after taking several sips of the delicious thin soup.

"What do you mean, Your Majesty?" he asked guardedly.

"Only a man of great courage would save a Princess from her own stupid pride by forcing her out of her carriage. . . especially into such. . . inclement weather," she said. She tried to sound angry but somehow her tone had no edge. Her gray eyes shimmered in the candle's light, golden dots dancing from the rays' reflection in her large glowing pupils. Then, inexplicably, she found herself smiling at him!

When Favo realized that she was teasing, his face turned crimson. He wanted to look away, to walk away, but instead he gazed into eyes that drew him down into a treacherous whirlpool of emotion. "Might such a man be brave enough to risk a King's wrath by kissing his eldest daughter?"

Volumina felt her heart skip a beat. This man was flirting with her! She knew she should have him arrested

for treason, but she wanted to see what would happen
next. In addition, she was not one to turn away from any
kind of verbal sparring, and certainly not now when this
felt more exciting than anything she had ever experienced. "What might be brave in one situation would be
foolhardy in another," she said coyly.

"Call it what you will," her bodyguard replied as he
touched her face gently with his hands, "but you are too
beautiful to resist."

Trembling slightly at the nearness of him, Volumina
closed her eyes as he kissed her. His lips were soft and
warm, his kiss chaste but holding the promise of so
much more if circumstances were different. She sighed
with disappointment when she heard her attendant
coming up the stairs. Favo heard it too and the spell was
broken. He quickly drew back, mumbled something
about seeing to his men, and left just as Marilee was
entering. Her face too was flushed, but not from ascend-
ing the steep staircase. She had been gone longer than
proper, being detained by a flirtatious encounter of her
own with Pozzi in the stableyard where she too had
been on the receiving end of a kiss that turned her
stomach to water.

The lady-in-waiting was no fool. Seeing the guilty look on Favo's face, she assessed the situation immediately. She liked and admired the handsome bodyguard, but this madness must be stopped at once. From now on, until they arrived at the Palace, she vowed not to let Volumina out of her sight.

"Members of the Court,

I have become aware

of a grave danger

that threatens the Kingdom."

Chapter 8

The winter blizzard subsided during the night, but not the storms raging within Volumina. She had let a man, a commoner at that, *KISS* her. And worse, she had enjoyed his attentions and was not sure she would have resisted his advances if the opportunity for things to get carried away had been there. One part of her thanked God that Marilee had returned when she did, another wished she had not. Thus despite the fact that she was much fatigued from the day, sleep did not come for a very long time. When it did, her dreams were filled with nightmares of her father finding out and visiting all manner of hideous punishments upon her bodyguard.

When Favo roused her from her fitful sleep at dawn by knocking loudly on her chamber door, Volumina was more physically exhausted than she had ever been in her young life. But upon hearing his voice, every cell of her body was on full alert. She had no appetite for food, but felt an empty longing inside she knew no sweetcake or buttercream candy would fill. She felt like a brazen hussy, but she could not deny she wanted to kiss him again, to wrap herself in the warmth of his massive arms. But when Marilee opened the door to tell him they would be ready within the hour, he was already gone.

With the welcome break in the weather, travel was faster and by late afternoon, the castle was in sight. Favo had busied himself with his official duties all day, and Marilee had stuck to her charge like sap to a tree. Volumina was happy to be home, but she was not sure exactly how to proceed once inside the castle. She had sent a messenger ahead to inform the King that an emergency necessitated her immediate return to Sveltelanna. She had asked that the Royal Family, the Advisory Council, and all the ministers be called to assembly that evening. She knew her parents would be gravely concerned about her welfare, and even more bewildered by her request, but she was sure her father trusted her enough to comply with her wishes. She had then spent the entire day alone with her thoughts, rehearsing the words she would use to convince the court that they must begin a kingdom-wide program of gathering, gleaning and rationing to avoid a disastrous famine that would cause suffering of a magnitude never before seen in Thynneland.

Upon arriving at the castle gates, the traveling party was met by a large honor guard dressed in black and crimson in tribute to the coming Christmas season. Volumina winced when she saw them. She remembered that her mother had ordered the soldier's coats and pants be decorated in pure spun gold, each uniform probably costing more than a year's worth of food for a hungry family. She was sure her parents knew nothing of the situation in the Hinterland. She herself had been insulated from such unpleasantries and had taken the excesses of the court for granted. Until Favo's astounding revelation, she had been completely oblivious to what the castle's upkeep, especially its pomp and ceremony, cost the common folk whose taxes supported it.

"Well, that was fine in times of plenty," she thought as they crossed the lowered drawbridge, "but when prosperity declines, so should spending on unnecessary frills. I shall speak of it with my father the first chance I get."

Once inside the castle walls, Pozzi carefully guided the horses to the palace door. Favo was right there to open the carriage door and help Volumina down the makeshift stairs, but he seemed cold and distant. Volumina had no way of knowing that, in truth, he was struggling to control his emotions, well aware of the electricity that passed between them as he took her hand to help her descend. She mistook his chilly demeanor as affirmation of her worst fears. He had merely been toying with her, playing a game of dares. She had been a fool to entertain the thought that he considered her attractive and desirable. Well, this was no time for self-flagellation. She must put this entire matter out of her mind; she had work to do.

Upon entering the Throne Room, the Princess caught the King's eye and smiled her thanks. Rollo and Reeda sat amid the entire assembled Court, which fell silent as Volumina, accompanied by a stern and silent Favo, strode confidently across the room and stood in front of her parents. Volumina noticed that even Demura was present, probably consumed by curiosity at her older sister's motives for coming home early and under such mysterious circumstances.

Volumina removed her heavy cloak and handed it to Favo, causing some members of the court to gasp in approval. The "portly" Princess was considerably slimmer! While she was certainly not yet thin, she could best be described as statuesque, her physical presence so imposing that absolute silence reigned in the room.

"Your Majesties," she began as she curtsied in front of her parents. "Members of the Court," she continued as she turned to acknowledge them. "As you can see, I have not yet completed my legislated Weight Reduction Program. I would still be in the Hinterland as directed had I not become aware of a grave danger that threatens the Kingdom. I am informed that Thynneland teeters on the brink of a great famine."

A gasp of shock went round the room as Volumina's news was digested by the crowd. Twirpin, the minister who had cruelly shouted to the crowd her humiliating personal statistics at her last weigh-in, blanched and tried to avoid her penetrating gaze.

"Should the Minister of Weights and Measures, whose duties include oversight of Food Production and Distribution, wish to interrupt my remarks, pray do so," she said, her eyes boring into Twirpin's very core.

Stunned and confused, he stood mute while she went on.

"Very well," she said in a clear, commanding voice. "It is well known in the Hinterland that drought has severely impacted this year's harvest. We can perhaps weather the crisis, but only if the Court immediately begins austerity measures, including mandatory food rationing and suspension of excise taxes. I challenge every single citizen of Thynneland to take it as his or her patriotic duty to support and abide by the Share-And-Share-Alike Act, which I shall present to the Court tomorrow for ratification. The new law dictates that those who have always enjoyed a position of privilege will be the first to tighten their belts."

Now elective dieting and forced food rationing may produce the same result but are viewed in completely different ways. Realizing what the Princess was proposing, the courtiers began to mutter and mumble. Suspension of taxes? Food rationing? Had her Weight Reduction Program addled her brain completely? The assemblage began giving voice to its complaints and the noise soon built to a crescendo.

"Silence!" roared the King, who now turned to the Minister of Weights and Measures. "How is it I have not been told of this?"

"Do not place the blame on me, Sire," Twirpin responded when he found his voice. "I myself was not aware of the severity of the shortages until this very morning. Indeed, when I was summoned to Court for the Princess's unexpected return, I was at my desk putting the finishing touches on the relevant report."

Favo sniffed disdainfully, and Volumina rolled her eyes, then ignored his transparent defense as she began speaking once more. "The Court must also suspend all but the most necessary purchases. All able-bodied men will be asked to help with hunting, food storage, and distribution, while women will assist in scavenging for wild edibles and preserving foods for later use."

"Those are some of the very measures I include in my proposal," the beleaguered minister began, but Rollo interrupted him. "Go, Twirpin. You are dismissed to complete your report. Have it ready on the morrow by the time I break my fast."

The Minister bowed deeply, then threw his nose in the air and drew his cloak tight as he hurried out, followed by his two assistants. All three would spend a sleepless night manufacturing a document necessary to keep them out of the King's dungeon.

"My Royal Daughter, duty requires me to ask you the name of the person from whom you received word of the impending disaster," Rollo said when Twirpin and his lackeys had gone. "It needs be a source we can trust, for this is someone in whose word we have now placed the future of our kingdom."

Volumina hesitated and then glanced at Favo, who had been staring at her but immediately looked away when she pointed him out. "From my loyal and faithful bodyguard, whose family abides in the southern area, which suffers most severely from the drought," Volumina replied. "I have found him to be a forthright and truthful servant, a man of the highest integrity."

Reeda, who had heretofore sat in silent awe of her daughter's magnificent performance, now entered the conversation. "I speak for the women of the court, Princess Volumina, when I say we accept your judgment in this matter. We stand willing to assist, but I can think of no woman in the palace experienced enough to teach the survival skills you say we must acquire and practice."

At this Favo too broke his silence. "Forgive me, Your Highness. My widowed mother is quite skilled in the art of subsistence. Perhaps she could be engaged to teach the women of the court. . ."

"Done. We need such a one as we can trust," Reeda replied. "Summon her to court immediately. She will move into the Palace and assume her duties at once."

"And you, Favo," the King added, "you are to be commended for your good and faithful service to the realm." At this Favo blushed and bowed deeply. "You have not only brought our beloved daughter home safely, but you have served the people well by supplying unpopular but critical information. When time permits, the court shall bestow the proper recognition for your heroism. For now, you shall continue in my service as Chief Deputy of Palace Security, acting as my personal bodyguard until further notice."

If this be the ways of love,

Volumina decided,

then love was much overrated.

Chapter 9

The next day Rollo and Volumina met at dawn to draft her proposal, a fair and equitable law governing the sale and distribution of food in Thynneland. The Share-And-Share-Alike Act forbade hoarding, price-gouging, smuggling and theft of any and all foodstuffs. The penalty for breaking the law was appropriate and just. Offenders would be cut to half-rations and sent to the countryside to forage for food until such time as the famine was declared legally over. All social events, such as leatherball games, were suspended until the crisis ended. Favo had no trouble convincing his teammates to volunteer their services. Each player would oversee one of the distribution crews that would deliver food parcels to the far reaches of the country.

Volumina, who had asked to take charge of the Food Procurement and Distribution Program, was determined to set a good example. Too busy to trifle with menu choices, she once again put Marilee in charge of her food intake. She must be served the minimum number of nutrients required to protect her health and keep up her strength, but not a morsel more. Real hunger now replaced appetite, but she felt her stomach satisfied by small portions of things she would never before have considered food. She found she liked the taste of wild seeds and nuts, especially ground acorns that had been shelled, boiled, mashed and mixed with her morning gruel. She continued to shed pounds but gain energy. She lost much weight in her face, a factor that revealed gorgeous high cheekbones and a long, slender neck that made her even more stunning.

This did not go unnoticed, especially by Favo who found himself physically aroused in her presence and thus went out of his way to avoid her. On one occasion, the two accidentally met in a narrow passageway leading to the Banquet Hall that had been designated Royal War-on-Famine Headquarters. In a hurry that morning and not paying attention, Volumina turned a corner and ran full force into him, resulting in their both falling in a tangled heap. Startled but unhurt, they sat on the cold stone floor for a moment. Then, as they began disentangling, Volumina started laughing at their clumsiness.

In the instant that Favo realized he was actually touching her, it was all he could do to keep himself from taking her in his arms and stopping her laughter with kisses. Luckily, he thought later, the moment was interrupted by the sound of approaching voices. Favo recognized one as that of his mother, Rosalie. Suddenly, he came to his senses. This woman he desired was a Royal and he a commoner. No matter how much he might wish it otherwise, for both his and his mother's sake, he must regard her as forbidden fruit never to be touched again. Stammering profuse apologies, he helped her to her feet and they went their separate ways undetected.

For her part, Volumina was left with conflicted feelings. On the one hand, she was sure Favo cared little for her. How could she think otherwise when he ignored and avoided her at every turn? And had he not called her fat, lazy and spoiled? Then why was it that just being near him excited and thrilled her beyond measure? If this be the ways of love, she decided, love was much overrated and she would not let such dangerous emotions take hold and torture her.

"That is not true, my daughter.

You have changed yourself;

the hardest task of all."

Chapter 10

On a cold, raw February day, Volumina and the King sat at a table engaged in discourse about how even the blackest cloud has a proverbial silver lining.

"The famine is a calamity, of course," Rollo remarked, "but the Share-and-Share-Alike Act has united our kingdom in a way I never thought possible."

"And Christmastide," Volumina observed, "our modest celebration allowed the true meaning to take its rightful place by filling our hearts with peace and love."

"Rightly said, my dearest daughter," Rollo answered. "And it fills my heart, if not my belly, to see that you and your mother have grown close during our time of trouble. Why, even your sister has shown her true noble mettle by working dawn to dusk in the food preservation kitchens."

Volumina smiled warmly, her intense gray eyes glowing with pride and affection. Then the conversation turned to more efficient ways of stretching their waning food stores, and they found themselves bemoaning the fact that they had taken the availability of unlimited food for granted and wasted so much of it in the past. They chided each other for their foolishness, recalling times of feasting until their stomachs ached, then exercising until near exhaustion to burn off the excess calories. Rollo covered his face in shame as Volumina reminded them both that members of the Royal Family had routinely ordered entire meals be thrown to the dogs simply because they were not in the mood for the cook's menu choices that evening.

Suddenly, for no apparent reason, Volumina had a flashback to her father's nocturnal visits. Remembering the delicious cakes and candies he'd brought her almost every night also called to mind a question she'd been pondering for some time. Now at last, she felt ready to ask it.

"Father," she began in a halting voice. "How is it I became a slave to my craving for sweet things? They were but a moment's pleasure on my lips that turned to pain as they transformed me into the Portly Princess."

"Much of the blame lies in me, my daughter," the King replied with unexpected honesty. There was also a tone of humility in his clear, baritone voice that Volumina had never heard before. "Because I myself found such foods pleasurable, I thought that giving you sweet things would bind us together more closely. By the time I realized my actions were merely bribery of the cruelest kind, it was too late. Your habits had formed and you were no longer in control."

"You are a kind, decent man, and otherwise a good father," Volumina replied softly. "I would have loved you anyway."

"Perhaps, but how could I know that?" he asked. "Then, in the years that followed, I compounded my transgressions by allowing you to continue eating unrestrained. You were headstrong and stubborn and it was easier to just give in to your tantrums than to do what I knew in my heart was right. I rationalized and excused my behavior until the anniversary of your eighteenth birth date when the results of my folly were on display for all the kingdom to see."

Volumina went over and put her arms around her father in an unmistakable gesture of forgiveness. "I understand you better now," she said, "and I wouldst you had acted differently. But that is water under the river bridge, and we cannot change what is."

The King embraced Volumina and then held her away from him. "That is not true, my daughter. You have changed yourself; that is the hardest task of all."

Her father's complimentary words filled and satisfied Volumina as not even the most sumptuous meal could ever do, and she felt the time was right to ask her one remaining question. "What of my mother's role in the matter of my obesity?"

"Your mother tried her best, but I undermined and thwarted her efforts until she gave up in despair," the King admitted. "Do not place blame at her feet, my daughter. She suffers enough, grieving and chastising herself for asking God to accomplish what she could not. Your mother chafes at the irony: God has finally, and cruelly, answered her prayers. You have grown thinner than she could have ever imagined. But it does not make her happy, for it comes by forced deprivation in the service of our people."

Volumina pondered his words before replying. "And now Thynneland's fate is also in the hands of God," she said. "Let us hope He has no more cruel surprises in store."

"We present this gift,

requiring as our only payment

a private audience with King Rollo."

Chapter 11

Had the Share-and-Share-Alike Act been implemented at the end of summer, it might have gotten Thynneland through until the new growing season. However, since it had not taken shape until mid-December, the Kingdom's food stores were nearly exhausted by the first of March. The farm animal herds had been culled to near-dangerous levels, with only a small number of cows, pigs, sheep and chickens spared to replenish their livestock the next summer. Every edible known to be safe for human consumption: wild game, grains, nuts, berries, roots and stalks; had been hunted and gathered. Nothing was wasted, with Rollo and Volumina working tirelessly to stretch their provisions as far as possible. But finally, they admitted they would not have enough. Volumina suggested they send a delegation to the distant Kingdom of Hollsteene where adequate rain had fallen, and Rollo's second cousin by marriage, King Hilliard, reportedly had food to sell.

Rollo resisted. He and Hilliard had become estranged after the Hollsteene Hogskins had thrashed the Thynneland Whackers in the Leatherball Championship Game two decades ago, a fierce competition that sent Thynneland's great running back Greeno to an early retirement. However, Volumina convinced the King the situation was growing desperate and this was no time for foolish pride or old grudges. Rollo reluctantly agreed. Knowing he must send someone he could trust, the King chose Favo and Pozzi, who were dispatched immediately with the kingdom's last bag of gold, enough to buy two months' worth of provisions.

On a crisp but sunny late March afternoon, when Volumina wept silently as she oversaw the loading and dispatch of food wagons containing the last of their stores, Favo and Pozzi returned, leading a wagon caravan heaped high with welcome sacks of wheat, oats and corn. Overjoyed to see that they had accomplished their mission, she waved excitedly to them from the parapet. Pozzi saluted smartly, but Favo looked away and did not return her greeting. The two had not been alone together since their accidental meeting in the passageway, but she had been accustomed to having him about the Palace and found that she had missed him while he was gone.

Riding some distance behind the procession were several men she did not recognize, a fact that surprised her. She thought herself acquainted with nearly everyone in Thynneland, especially since she had visited every village and hamlet in her quest to keep the wolf from her subjects' doors. Upon closer inspection, she recognized them to be sporting Hollsteene's colors and hurried down to tell her father.

She found the King already at the castle gates, formally greeting Hilliard, whom he had not seen in twenty years. Volumina stood watching in amazement as a herald blew his trumpet and addressed the gathering crowd. "King Hilliard and Prince Brayno of Hollsteene present the citizens of Thynneland with this gift of food, requesting as their only payment a private audience with their second cousin by marriage, King Rollo."

"Apparently bygones are bygones," Volumina thought as she examined the pair. Hilliard was a tall bearded man with a massive upper body and muscular thighs, brown curly hair and dark brown eyes. His look was somehow familiar to her, but she could not place it so she turned her attention to the Prince. Brayno was thin, but fit, his hair and skin the color of the wheat the soldiers were busy unloading even as they spoke. She guessed his age to be about sixteen. The most attractive thing about the Prince was his face, which advertised the intellectual acumen his name aptly implied.

"We humbly accept your kind gift, Your Highnesses," Rollo said in response, "and are honored to have you as our guests. How goes it with our fair cousin, Queen Whinafred?"

Volumina was surprised to hear her father ask. He had often given her the impression he bore no affection for Whinafred, who was widely reputed to be an ill-tempered scold.

"Alas," King Hilliard said, his face adopting a forlorn look that somehow wasn't quite as sad as it should have been. "We thought you would have had word by now. My queen died of a fever just before the turning of the new year and now enjoys her eternal reward in heaven." Volumina thought King Hilliard's tone contained more relief than grief, but Brayno's eyes welled with tears at the mention of the loss of his mother.

"Our deep condolences to you both," Rollo replied. Hilliard and Brayno bowed in acknowledgment of Rollo's expression of sympathy, and Volumina thought it best to lift the somber mood by changing the subject.

"My personal attendant, Marilee, will see to your immediate needs, and the Royal Family shall meet with you tomorrow morning when you are refreshed from a good night's rest," she said, taking charge.

"Excellent," King Hilliard replied. "Our needs are few. We require sleeping quarters, a simple dinner, and stabling for our horses. That will be sufficient."

"Done," Rollo said. "Until the morrow," he added, and both kings bowed to one another in mutual respect.

"I will marry you,

Prince Brayno,

if you will have me."

Chapter 12

The requested audience began late the next morning. Rollo, Reeda, Volumina and Demura were seated on chairs reserved for formal occasions, while Hilliard and Brayno sat opposite on a hastily erected platform. The only other people in the room were a scribe who would record the meeting and Pozzi and Favo who were standing guard in full armor at the door.

For some reason, Volumina was nervous. "No gift is truly free," she mused, "there are always strings attached. What does King Hilliard want in return for his generous bequest?" She decided to just sit quietly; she would find out soon enough.

Rollo began by once again thanking his cousin. "We are most grateful for this gift of life for Thynneland, King Hilliard. We hope someday to be able to repay your generosity."

"Under the circumstances, it was the right thing for us to do," Hilliard replied with a condescending smile that did not escape Volumina's notice. She also saw that Brayno was amusing himself with a small puzzle, which he quickly hid in his sleeve whenever his father looked his way.

"But for you and the Prince to accompany the grain wagons. . . that is unprecedented," Rollo responded, apparently as eager as Volumina to learn if his cousin had ulterior motives for the unexpected visit.

"Set your mind at ease, my royal cousin. I am not here to propose a rematch of our last athletic contest." Rollo winced and Hilliard laughed, then took on a more serious tone as he went on. "No, this would not be the time for such frivolity. I am here because, like Thynneland, Hollsteene has a void that must be filled. My son Brayno comes of marriage age in less than two years and we have been unable to find a suitable match for him."

"And. . . " King Rollo said, encouraging Hilliard to continue.

"And. . . I have been told you have an exceptionally beautiful daughter who is also in need of a suitable marriage partner." He looked straight at Volumina.

Rollo seemed not to be following the conversation at first, but upon realizing what Hilliard was getting at, said a bit sharply, "Tell me straight what it is you propose."

"I wish to betroth my son Brayno to your eldest daughter, Volumina. It seems the perfect match. For Hollsteene it ensures that our line of succession continues; for Thynneland it guarantees generous economic assistance until the kingdom is able to recover from the ravages of famine and once again support itself."

Volumina felt her knees grow weak. She looked to her father, her mother, to Favo for deliverance. Her parents were whispering, but their facial expressions seemed to indicate more than polite interest in Hilliard's proposal. Favo's face, well hidden by his helmet, did not appear to have changed one iota. Only Pozzi was aware that, upon hearing the visitor's words, Favo had slumped toward the wall and been forced to steady himself by grabbing the door frame. Now he stood still as a statue, as if any motion might blow him to pieces like shattered crystal.

Volumina felt that she was signing her own death sentence, but during the past few months she had come to love her country more than herself. If Thynneland's future security could be so easily purchased, it was more than worth whatever personal sacrifice she must make. "The choice is not mine," she thought, "but since I cannot have the man I love, then I will learn to love the man I have."

"I think the match a good one," she declared in as steady a voice as she could muster, "but first I must seek Brayno's view on the matter." She got up, walked over and looked hard at the young Prince who rose to acknowledge her.

"What think you about this proposed marriage?" she asked.

Even at full dress height, Brayno barely reached Volumina's chin. In answering her question, he looked her up and down with only a modicum of interest. "You're too tall and thin, your voice is too loud, and you are much too self-possessed, but you're pretty enough. I am not fussy. If I must have a wife, you will do."

The two monarchs were about to clasp hands to cement the deal when Demura, who had sat as if invisible throughout the deliberations, rose and ran to Brayno's side. "No!" she cried. "Volumina only agrees to the match in order to assure the kingdom's future. She is the one who has done the lion's share of work in saving Thynneland. Now it is my turn."

She took the Prince's hand and peered deeply into his intelligent eyes. "I will marry you, Prince Brayno, if you will have me," she said in a sweet, humble voice. "You will not be sorry if you choose me instead of my sister. You discerned rightly. She is too loud and bossy. And, in truth, I like the looks of you."

The Prince seemed pleased by the fact that he now had a choice and felt more than flattered by Demura's last remark. He sensed at once that he would be far more comfortable with the younger sister as his bride. "Do you like books? Puzzles? Games?" Brayno suddenly asked.

"Oh, indeed!" Demura responded enthusiastically. "Volumina likes them not." She turned her nose up at her sister. "Her life is so monotonous. She does nothing all day but attend court, administer justice, and travel about the kingdom intermingling with the peasants."

"Then I choose. . . you," Brayno said, taking Demura's hand and gallantly escorting her back to her chair before positioning himself directly in front of Rollo. "May I have the honor of petitioning the King for your youngest daughter's hand in marriage?" he said in a very regal voice.

At a loss for words by what he had just witnessed, Rollo could only manage a nod of acceptance.

"Well done!" Hilliard shouted gleefully, grabbing Rollo's hand and pulling him in for a huge bear hug. "I know it is forbidden, but just this once let us celebrate with a cup of wine, my cousin. I brought a bottle with me in hopes of using it to toast our new alliance."

Rollo looked at Reeda, who gave him an "all right, but just this once" look, then rang the servant's bell. When Rosalie appeared at the door, Favo smiled weakly at his mother, who had been rewarded by her exemplary service during the famine with the coveted post of Overseer of Castle Hospitality.

Calling to her from across the room, King Hilliard instructed her to hurry to his quarters to fetch the precious vintage hidden in his personal baggage. She returned a few minutes later with a tray containing a bottle of Bordeaux and six silver goblets. Carefully pouring a tiny amount in four of the goblets and topping off the other two, she began by serving Reeda first, then Demura, then Volumina. She carefully averted her eyes when she passed a goblet to Brayno and almost turned completely to the side when she handed one of the full vessels to Hilliard. Finally, she handed the other full goblet to Rollo.

"Thank you, Rosalie," Volumina said as the servant hurried to the door.

"Rosalie?" Hilliard suddenly said, repeating her name.

"Yes, my Lord?" she replied, turning to see who had called her name.

"Rosalie. . . of Hiltonshire in northern Hollsteene? Can it possibly be?" He motioned for her to come forward and she reluctantly obeyed.

"What is it you wish, my lord?" she said, trembling as she stood before him.

He came down to her and gently took her face in his huge hands. "Look at me, Rosalie," he insisted. She did as he commanded, but there was trepidation in her expression as she finally looked him full in the face.

"It is you, Rosalie," he said, as the tears welled up in his dark eyes.

"Yes, my lord," she whispered as he drew her to him. Everyone else in the room was too shocked to comprehend what was happening or even attempt a response. Favo's jaw had dropped when Hilliard had first called Rosalie's name, and it remained open throughout the ensuing scene.

Hilliard continued to hold her close and speak as if he and Rosalie were long-lost lovers. "Why did you run away?

Where did you go? I searched everywhere for you. I wanted to tell you I had secured my father's acceptance of the match!"

"But we were so young, my lord, and I would not force you into an unsuitable union you might some day regret because of my. . . situation." Rosalie blushed and Hilliard finally learned the secret she had been carrying for almost a quarter century.

"You. . . you were with child? Rosalie, why did you not tell me?" She did not or could not answer, so he continued, his voice trembling as he asked the question they all had on the tip of their tongues. "Rosalie, what happened to the issue of our young love's illicit union?"

"He stands guard at the door, my lord," she replied, and looked with eyes full of love at her son Favo.

At this news, an involuntary gasp escaped Volumina's lips. From the corner of her eye, she saw Favo's knees buckle. He would have fallen had not Pozzi caught him as he fell unconscious into his best friend's arms.

Fairy tales

always end happily,

and this one is no exception.

Chapter 13

After being roused from his faint, Favo was escorted to the Royal Reading Room for a private audience with his mother, father, and half-brother where the story was soon told. Young Prince Hilliard of Hollsteene and Rosalie of Rottendam had fallen in love during the Princess's first visit to the Hollsteene Summer Faire. Unfortunately, Hilliard's father was not in favor of the match. Instead, he betrothed Hilliard to Princess Whinafred of Crabbridge.

The two lovers had met secretly in a deserted wood-cutter's cottage to devise a plan to thwart the proposed marriage, a rendezvous during which unreined passion had led to Rosalie's predicament. But the King was adamant; Hilliard would marry Whinafred.

Upon learning that she was with child, a shamed and hopeless Rosalie had disguised herself as a peasant and fled Hollsteene. She found refuge and employment in a rectory in a tiny village in faraway Thynneland, vowing to keep the truth locked in her heart forever. Like the villagers and the friar for whom she kept house, Rosalie told Favo she had been widowed and Favo orphaned when his father had met his death at the hands of a careless hunter whose stray arrow had pierced his heart.

"Princess Rosalie," Hilliard stated with firm resolution once everything had been explained, "we no longer have reason to hide the truth. Whinafred has gone to heaven, my son Brayno is to wed the Princess Demura, and my bed is cold and lonely. You should now rightly take your place by my side. Hollsteene, and I, need a Queen, that is, if you agree it is finally time for us to complete the match."

"Yes, my lord," Rosalie replied, her eyes filled with devotion for the man she had never stopped loving. "But I think it best to ask the blessing of my son, Prince Favo."

They turned to Favo, who was gallantly attempting to swim the tide of rising new emotions brought on by life-altering revelations. With questions he had silently carried all his life now answered, Favo nodded his approval, accepting his newfound family by embracing a father and half-brother he had not known existed.

The happy news was announced and two days later King Rollo and King Hilliard sat down to chart the merger of their kingdoms. It was determined that Prince Favo's gifts would be better utilized as future sovereign of Hollsteene, and Brayno's talents would be best suited for Thynneland. The half-brothers were consulted and the harmony of agreement reigned. At the younger prince's suggestion, Brayno was to be allowed to remain in Thynneland. He already felt comfortable in the palace and also seemed quite taken with Princess Demura. It was agreed that he and his betrothed would travel to Hollsteene for the annual Summer Faire, well-chaperoned, of course. They would be married two years and some months hence at Christmastide.

Within the week, Favo was packed and ready to accompany Hilliard and Rosalie back to Hollsteene. As Favo carried the last of his meager possessions to the oxcart in the courtyard, a much-worn leatherball fell from his bag. As he retrieved it, something caught his eye and he looked up at the castle window just in time to catch a glimpse of Volumina working in the War-on-Famine

Room. She wore a modest gray gown that Rosalie had taken in four times to fit the Princess's shrinking frame. Her still shiny ebony hair hung loosely to her thin waist. He had not seen the Princess since that fateful day in the Throne Room. She had spent every waking hour directing the distribution of grain to the outlying villages, while he had spent his time with Hilliard discussing his new realm's future.

His behavior dictated more by emotion than intellect, Favo impetuously decided to bid the Princess farewell. He strode quickly to the War-on-Famine Room where he found her finishing a scroll upon which she had written final directions for the disbursement teams.

"Princess Volumina. . ." he began. Startled, she looked up from her work to see his handsome, rugged face blushing. "I camest to bid you adieu. . . and to give you this." He walked over and pulled the leatherball from his cloak and placed it in her not quite steady hand. "Princess, I present this token as a vow that nothing as insignificant as a game shall ever again divide our two kingdoms."

"That is a most welcome promise, Prince Favo," Volumina stammered. "I know my father will be glad to hear of your kind gesture. He has said that when

Thynneland comes upon better days, he shall again sponsor a leatherball team. Perhaps at that time he may journey to Hollsteene to resume our now friendly rivalry."

"I wouldst be pleased should the Princess accompany King Rollo," Favo said in a sincere tone.

"You flatter me, but my journey there is not likely, Prince Favo," she replied, sure she was looking for the last time into the eyes of the man she would always love. She gazed at him for a long while, attempting to memorize his every feature, then cast her eyes down at his memento. He had called the game of leatherball "insignificant," but that was not true, for it had brought him to Thynneland and to her. "I am sure you will quickly forget your years here in Thynneland."

"Perhaps, but I shall never forget you, Princess," he replied huskily and once again, without meaning to, he took her in his arms and kissed her. She was so thin now, nothing but skin and bones, and it felt as if he might crush her if he held her as tightly as he wanted. Yet her lips were full and lush and he suddenly realized something he must have known from the first moment he had held her: there was so much strength, so much substance to her, and it was the kind that no scale could measure. He could

not explain it, but he felt it, and he no longer cared if she was fat or thin, ugly or beautiful. She was the woman he loved, and he would move heaven and earth to hold her like this forever.

Epilogue

Fairy tales always end happily, and this one is no exception. Thynneland enjoyed an abundant harvest during the next growing season, and the kingdom celebrated with Prince Favo making Princess Volumina his bride on the evening of the full harvest moon. She had regained a healthy amount of weight and looked stunning in her size 8 wedding gown. In the year following the wedding, Volumina gained almost thirty pounds, but lost most of it in one night when she gave birth to their baby daughter, Fullicia. They had agreed from the very start that Fullicia would be raised on a common-sense, healthy regimen, and of course, they all lived happily ever after.

Afternote

Let it be known that a royal decree was published soon after Fullicia's christening: King Rollo was NOT to be left alone with his new granddaughter, especially if he carried on his person even a single buttercream candy!